CAPTAIN FANTASTIC
and the Hullabaloo
at the Great Space Zoo

by Tommy Balaam
illustrations by Josh O'Brien

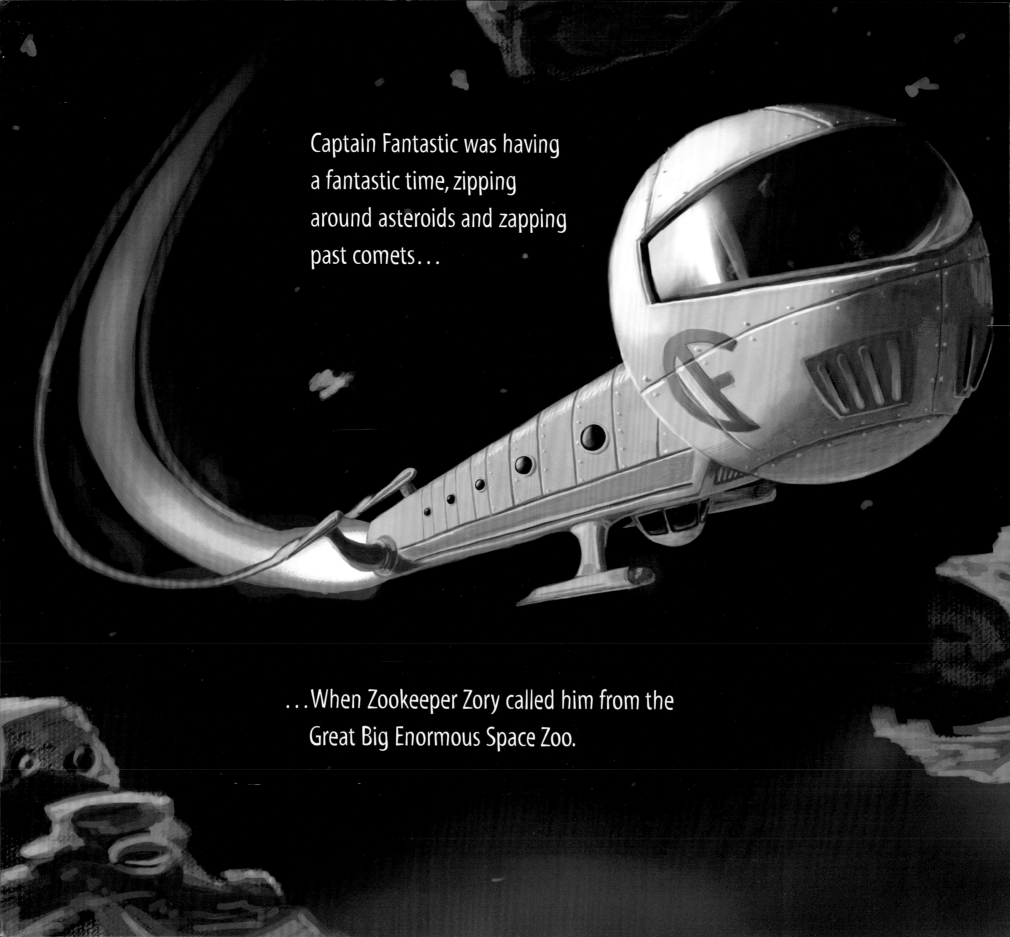

Captain Fantastic was having
a fantastic time, zipping
around asteroids and zapping
past comets...

...When Zookeeper Zory called him from the
Great Big Enormous Space Zoo.

The Captain zoomed to the Great Big Enormous Space Zoo.

"Don't worry, Zory," he said. "I'll find your animals!"

"Yippee!" said Zory. "I'd better go and feed the floogaloos."

Zory hurried off.

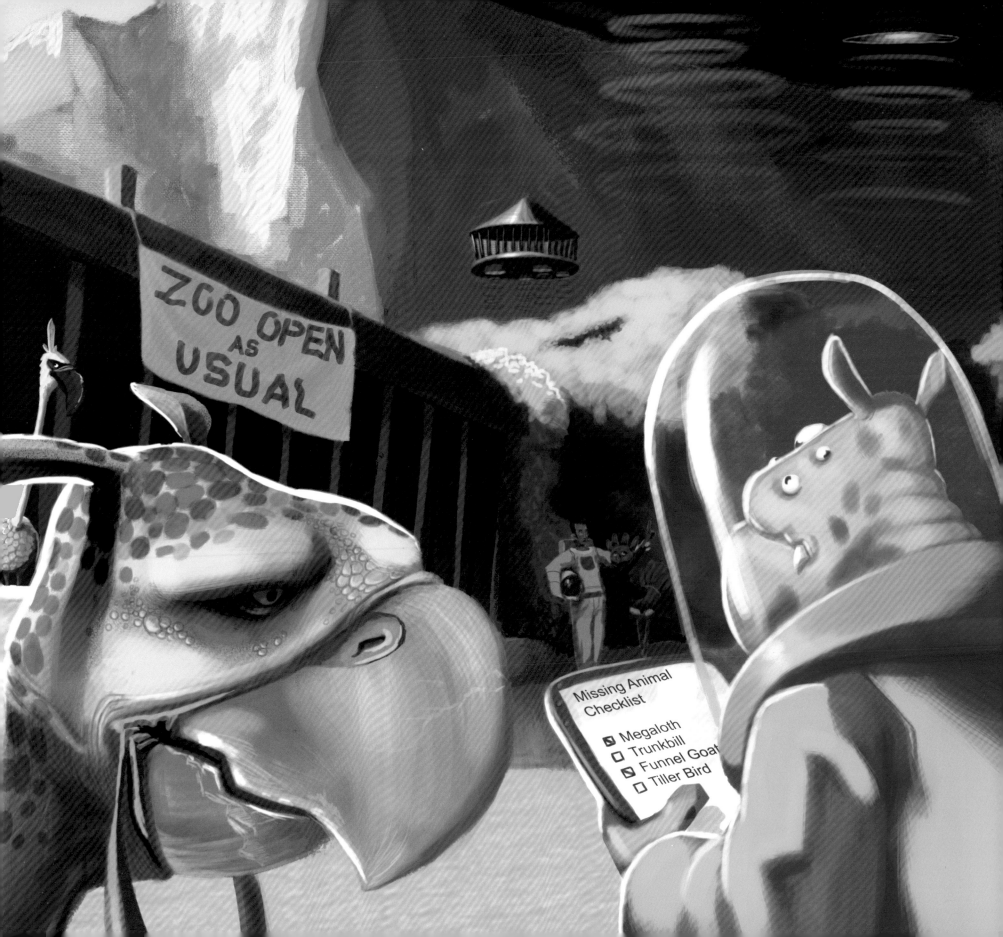

Captain Fantastic looked around, wondering how to find the missing animals.

"I know," he said. "I'll disguise myself as a blue space monkey, and if a horrible zoo-napper arrives I'll call the space police in a tickety-tock!"

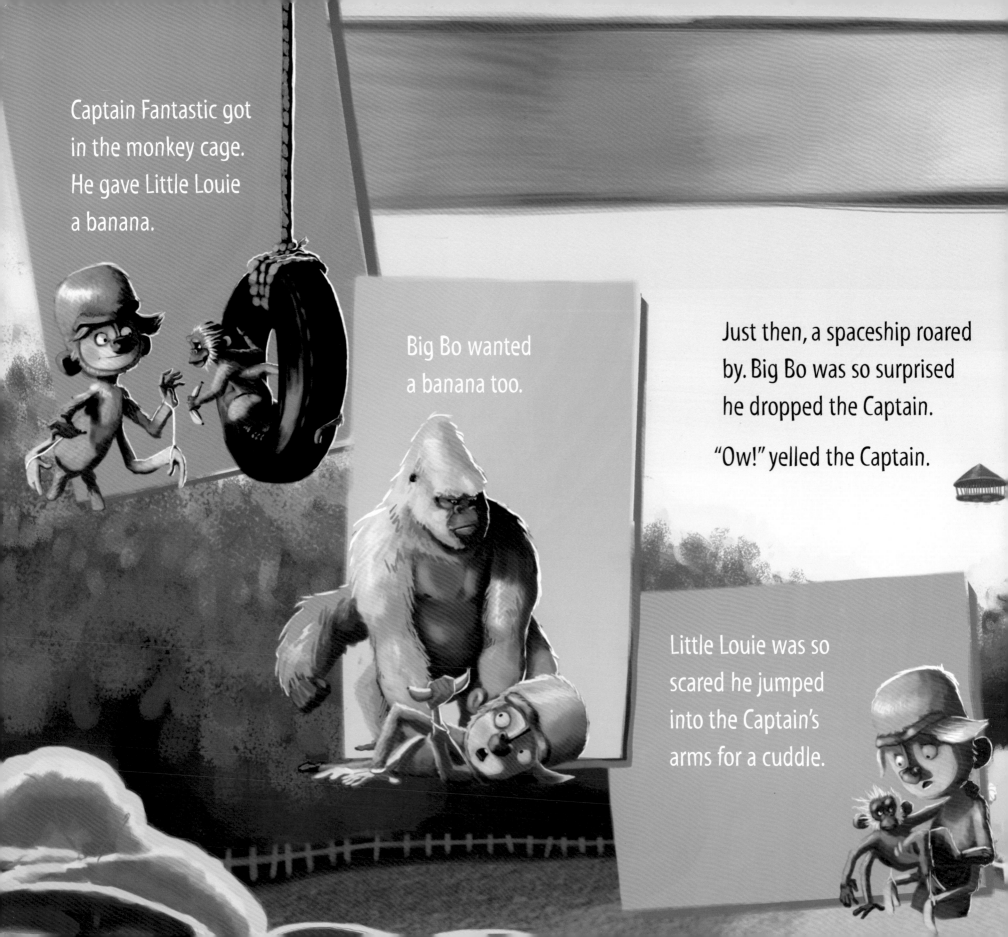

Captain Fantastic got in the monkey cage. He gave Little Louie a banana.

Big Bo wanted a banana too.

Just then, a spaceship roared by. Big Bo was so surprised he dropped the Captain.

"Ow!" yelled the Captain.

Little Louie was so scared he jumped into the Captain's arms for a cuddle.

SHLOOOOOP!

A ray of light zapped out of the spaceship and sucked them all up.

BUMP!

Captain Fantastic landed in the spaceship.

"Jumping jets!" he said. "That's Doctor Zob! He's the nastiest, naughtiest, ice cream swiping, chocolate-napping villain in the whole universe."

Captain Fantastic thought for a moment. "But I wonder why he wants the zoo animals?" he said to himself.

Doctor Zob picked up a Venusian flop-cat. "My super-duperiser ray will make you supersized and super brainy," he said.

KERZINGGGG!

A ray zapped out and the flop-cat got bigger and bigger.

"Hooray!" said Doctor Zob. "Now you can help me steal all the chocolate!"

"That sounds like hard work," said the flop-cat. "I think I'll take a nap instead." And it did.

Doctor Zob pointed at the Captain.
"Fetch that monkey, Winston,"
he said to the dog.

Winston licked the
Captain's face.

"Bad dog," Doctor Zob
shouted. "Stop being
good this minute!"

"Don't yell at him," said the Captain.
"He's only being
friendly."

"You be quiet! You're just a monkey!" Doctor Zob
shouted. "Wait a minute," he said. "Monkeys can't talk."

He pulled the Captain's mask off.

"Oops!" said the Captain.

Ooops!

Doctor Zob pulled out
a gloopy gun.

"This is a stick up," he said,
and pointed the gun at
the Captain.

"Just hold the monkey
for a minute," said
Captain Fantastic.

"I can't hold everything!"
yelled Doctor Zob.

"Here, let me help you,"
said the Captain.

He took the gloopy
gun off Doctor Zob.

"I don't like guns," said the Captain.

He put the gloopy gun down.

Big Bo picked the gun up and pointed it at the Captain and Little Louie.

Little Louie stuck his finger in the barrel of the gun. It made a whirring noise that got louder, and louder, and louder...

...and then it exploded!

Gloop him!

"You can be my bodyguard instead of that lazy cat," Doctor Zob said to Big Bo.
He pointed at the machine. "Prepare to be super-duperised!"

Big Bo went over to the machine. He dragged Captain Fantastic with him. He couldn't help it. They were stuck together with gloop!

Doctor Zob pushed a big red button.

ZZZINNGG!

The super-duperiser ray flashed down towards Big Bo and Captain Fantastic.

Winston tried to push Captain Fantastic out of the way.
That meant he pushed Big Bo too.

They all fell down in a heap.

The ray missed Captain
Fantastic, but it hit Big Bo's
bottom. It hit Winston too.

"Woof!" Winston said.
"Woo... Woohoo! I can talk!
And I'm big! Look, everyone!
I'm big!"

"Duh! I can talk too," said Big Bo.
"And my bottom is big."

"You can help me," Doctor Zob said to Big Bo. "We'll steal all the chocolate and all the ice cream too!"

"Oh my stars and comets!" said the Captain. "That doesn't sound fantastic. We have to stop them."

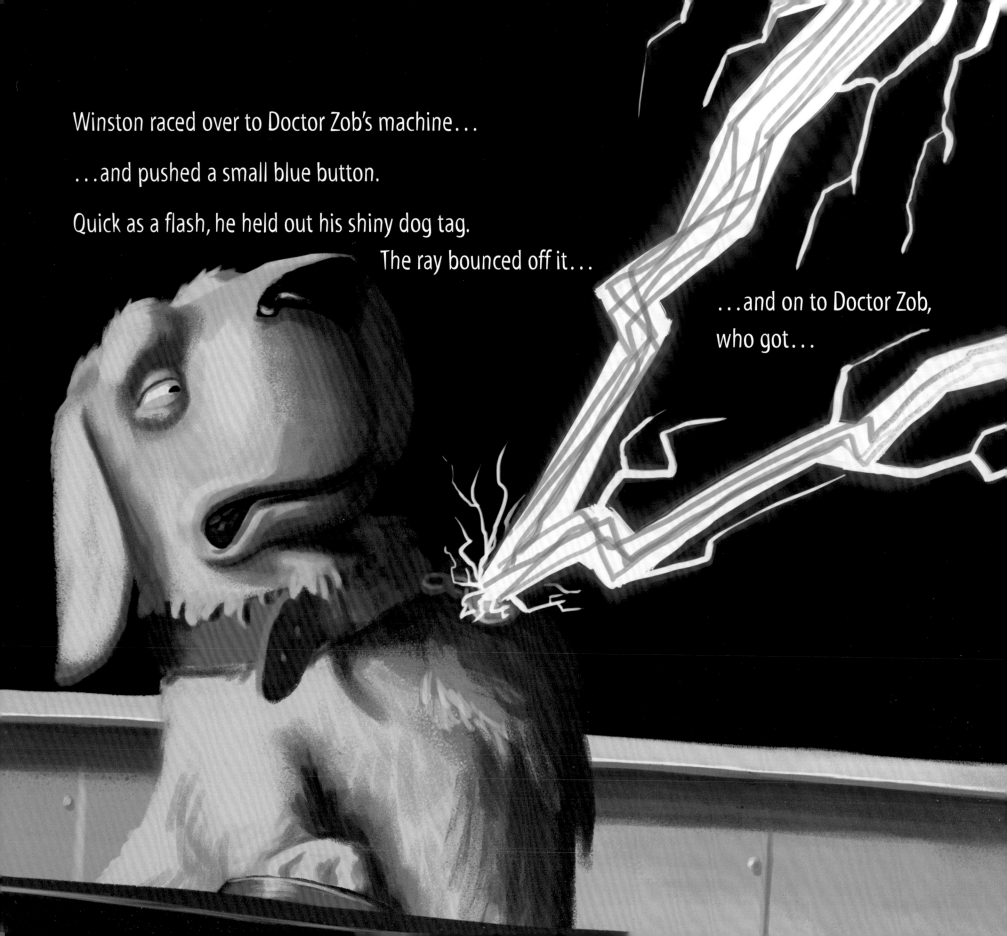

Winston raced over to Doctor Zob's machine…

…and pushed a small blue button.

Quick as a flash, he held out his shiny dog tag.

The ray bounced off it…

…and on to Doctor Zob,
who got…

. . .smaller
and smaller
and smaller.

Winston picked him up and popped him
into the flop-cat's cage.

Captain Fantastic took everyone back to the zoo.

"Please make me big again," begged Doctor Zob.

"Not until you've had a chance to learn your lesson," Winston said.

"I've learned my lesson," said Big Bo. "I'm clever now. I can talk! I like talking. And I like my bum being big. Please don't make it small again."

"I don't have to make it small," Winston said. He sounded worried. "I don't have to make myself small either, do I, Captain?"

"Sizzling skyrockets!" said Captain Fantastic. "Of course you don't!"

Zookeeper Zory called Constable Flumble, who took Doctor Zob and Big Bo to the Space Police station.

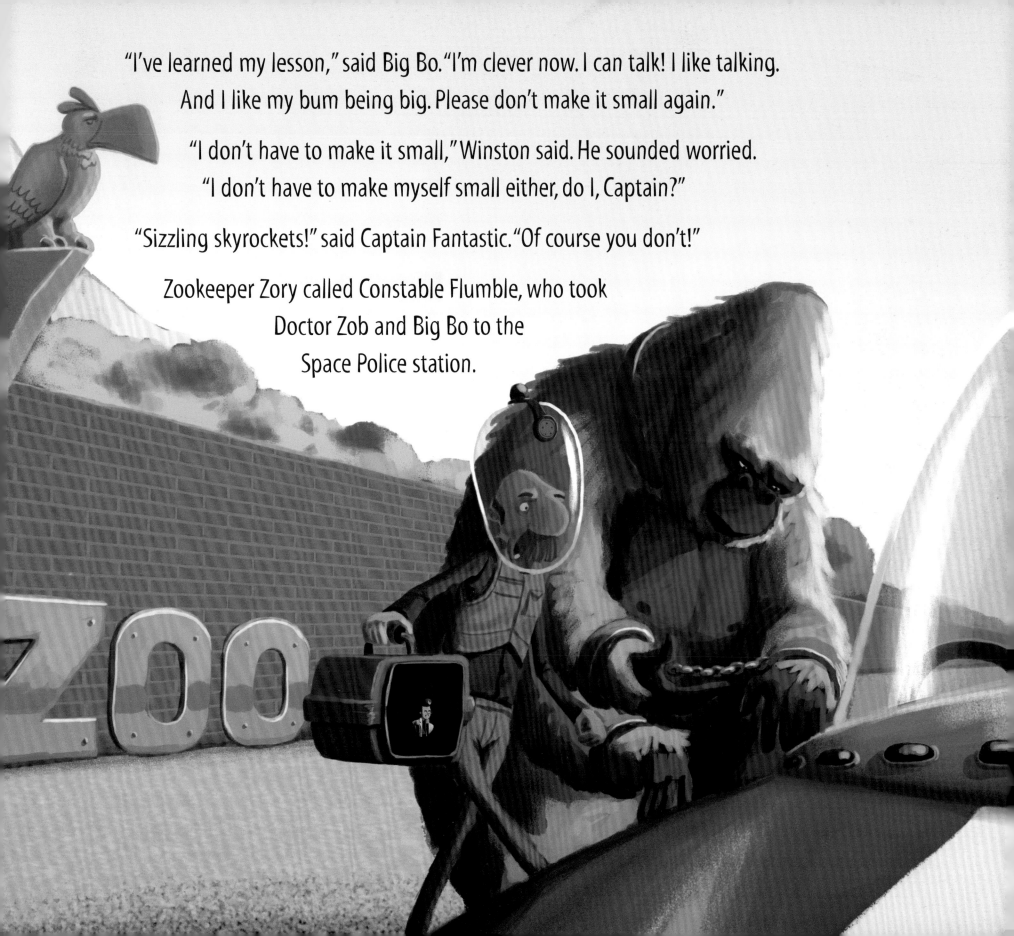

"What are you going to do now, Winston?" Zory asked. "You could work at the zoo, if you like."

"Thank you," said Winston. He turned to Captain Fantastic. "But what I'd really like is to have adventures with you in your spaceship."

"That would be fantastic," said the Captain.

And it was.